Robert Quackenbush

Surfboard to Peril

A Miss Mallard Mystery

•

Prentice-Hall, Inc.

Englewood Cliffs, New Jersey

Printed in Spain by Novograph, S.A., Madrid   ·J

Prentice-Hall International (UK) Limited, London
Prentice-Hall of Australia, Pty. Ltd., Sydney
Prentice-Hall Canada, Inc., Toronto
Prentice-Hall Hispanoamericana, S.A., Mexico
Prentice-Hall of India Private Ltd., New Delhi
Prentice-Hall of Japan, Inc., Tokyo
Prentice-Hall of Southest Asia Pte. Ltd., Singapore
Whitehall Books Limited, Wellington, New Zealand
Editora Prentice-Hall do Brasil LTDA., Rio de Janeiro

10 9 8 7 6 5 4 3 2 1

Library of Congress Cataloging in Publication Data

Quackenbush, Robert M.
    Surfboard to peril.

    Summary: While surfing in Hawaii, world-famous
Miss Mallard launches into one of her most dangerous
cases, one which involves the ownership of sacred
land and leads to kidnapping, mistaken identities,
bribery, blackmail, and death-defying chases.
    [1. Mystery and detective stories. 2. Ducks—
Fiction. 3. Hawaii—Fiction] I. Title.
PZ7.Q16Su 1986   [Fic]   85-24430
ISBN 0-13-877986-4

For Piet

While surfing in Hawaii, Miss Mallard —the world-famous ducktective—hit a large stone with her surfboard. She was tossed hard on the sand and just missed being run over by a bulldozer.

"Watch where you're going!" yelled the driver as he raced by without stopping.

Two young Hawaiians, who were gathering coconuts from nearby palm trees, saw the trouble and came running. Their names were Naku-Naku and Mori-Hi. They had taught Miss Mallard how to surf.

"Are you all right, Miss Mallard?" asked Naku-Naku.

"Just a bit shaken," replied Miss Mallard. "My surfboard hit a large stone. But I'm wondering why the driver of that bulldozer didn't stop."

"That's Clyde Pochard for you," said Mori-Hi. "He's a builder. He only thinks of himself and his condominiums. He is the reason Naku-Naku's family and my family are bitter enemies. He wants my family to sell the beachfront property between our villages. Naku-Naku's family says my family has no right to sell because the land is also theirs. However, my family has an old chart that says the land is ours. That is what the feud is all about. Still, it hasn't kept Naku-Naku and me from being friends just because our families don't get along."

While Mori-Hi and Miss Mallard were talking, Naku-Naku went to have a look at the stone Miss Mallard hit with her surfboard.

"Mori-Hi!" he cried. "Come have a look!"

Mori-Hi ran to Naku-Naku and the two friends began jumping up and down with excitement. Then they picked up the stone from the shallow water and brought it to shore.

Miss Mallard looked at the stone and saw that it was covered with ancient carvings and symbols.

"What is it?" she asked, puzzled.

"This is the sacred stone of our ancestors," said Mori-Hi. "It is written in our legends that our ancient ancestor Good King Huminhamin placed it on a pedestal on the very land I told you about. Then a great tidal wave came and swept it away, leaving an empty pedestal that still stands. The stone is older than my family's chart. It proves that both our families own the land."

"Lucky for us a wave brought it back after all this time and you found it, Miss Mallard," said Naku-Naku. "We must tell our families the news and replace the stone on its pedestal. From now on, neither family will be able to sell the land without the other family's consent."

They all went together to the pedestal. Naku-Naku and Mori-Hi placed the stone in its rightful place. Then Naku-Naku picked up a conch shell and blew it, "Aaaaawooooooo!"

"What a useful shell!" said Miss Mallard. "I found one like it on the beach today. I may use it to call taxis when I'm back in London."

All up and down the beach folks came running at the sound of the conch. They gathered around the pedestal. The leaders of the two villages stepped forward and when they saw the stone they were ashamed. They were reminded of their ancient heritage and their mutual ancestor the Good King Huminhamin. They were sorry they had quarreled and made peace.

"We must promise never to sell the land," said the leader of Naku-Naku's village. "We shall keep it for future generations."

"Agreed," said the leader of Mori-Hi's village. "Now let's have a feast."

"Hooray!" everyone shouted.

While the villagers were preparing for the feast—or luau—the news about the recovery of the legendary stone spread far and wide. Clyde Pochard was the first to hear the news and he came tearing down the beach in his bulldozer. Everyone could tell he was furious because he had lost his chance to buy the land. He honked his horn and splattered them with sand as he went by.

Then came two curiosity seekers who were pestering everyone to have a look at the stone. One was Horace Shoveller, a scientist who dug for ancient Hawaiian art pieces. The other was Joe Scaup, an old sailor who combed the beach for junk he could sell to tourists. They were promptly chased away.

At last the celebration began. A band played Hawaiian songs while dancers wearing grass skirts danced the "hula." Miss Mallard was invited to dance with the others. She caught on quickly to the steps and movements as though she had been wearing a grass skirt all her life.

Everyone danced until sunset and then they all sat down to a marvelous feast of pineapple, poi—a mashed root—and all sorts of other Hawaiian specialties. All during the feasting Miss Mallard was toasted frequently for finding the stone.

"Here's to Miss Mallard! Cheers to Miss Mallard!" everyone said as they held up their cups in unison.

After the feast everyone lit candles
and gathered around the stone to sing
goodnight songs. They hummed all the
way to the pedestal. But when they got
there, their hums changed to peals of
horror. The stone was not there!

"Call the police!" someone cried.

"No!" said the leader of Naku-Naku's
village. "The police would never believe
a story about a legendary stone that was
found, then lost again—all in one day."

"I agree," said the leader of Mori-Hi's
village. "We would all look foolish."

Miss Mallard stepped forward with
her knitting bag that contained her
detective kit.

"I'll investigate this case," she said.

Everyone stepped aside and Miss Mallard set to work. First she dusted the pedestal's base and looked for wingprints. There were none. Then she looked all around for footprints. They had all been brushed away. Then she examined the top of the pedestal where the stone had rested. She saw a clue! It was a keychain with a carving of a scary face dangling from it. It was carved from a shark's tooth.

Miss Mallard picked up the keychain and aimed a flashlight at it.

"Does anyone recognize this?" she asked.

All was quiet. Everyone shook their heads, "no."

"Well, then," said Miss Mallard. "Are there any suspects in this case?"

"What about Clyde Pochard?" someone said. "Everyone here saw him on the beach earlier. It would be to his advantage to take the stone so he could go ahead and buy the land."

This enraged the leaders of both villages.

"This would never have happened if you weren't so anxious to sell the land," said the leader of Naku-Naku's village.

"Don't point your wingtip at me," said the leader of Mori-Hi's village. "How do we know that you didn't take it yourself for some nutty reason?"

Naku-Naku and Mori-Hi looked at each other and shook their heads as if to say, "It's no use, the feuding has started all over again."

Miss Mallard spoke up and said, "Quarreling will not help us solve this case. Anyone could have taken the stone."

"You mean we're all suspects?" asked the two village leaders.

"Until this case is solved," replied Miss Mallard coolly. "Many of you were hopping up and down to fetch things during the feast, so you have weak alibis. I suggest that we all retire for the night. I'll give this case some thought and resume the investigation in the morning."

"Mori-Hi and I will walk back with you to your inn, Miss Mallard," said Naku-Naku.

Miss Mallard packed her tools and the keychain in her knitting bag while Naku-Naku and Mori-Hi lit a lantern. Then they left together on a path through the jungle. It was a short cut to Miss Mallard's inn.

The night was pitch black and there was a brisk wind whistling through the palm fronds. But as they walked they heard another sound, too. It was the sound of leaves and branches being crushed by footsteps. They were being followed!

"Run!" said Naku-Naku to Mori-Hi and Miss Mallard.

They ran as fast as they could and finally reached the inn. They had escaped their pursuer.

"Who was following us?" asked Miss Mallard, quite out of breath.

"I don't know," said Naku-Naku, "but we are not going back to find out. Mori-Hi and I will take the long way home along the beach."

"Let me get someone here to drive you home," said Miss Mallard. "I would feel much better about it."

She arranged at the hotel for someone to drive them home in a jeep. She stood on the front porch and watched them drive away. Then, just before she went inside, she shivered. She felt as if there were someone lurking in the jungle watching her. And waiting. She opened the door and ran to the safety of her room.

Miss Mallard made some notes about the case in her notebook. She wrote down all possible motives for the crime. Then she stared for a long time at the keychain. Finally, she put away her notes and the keychain and got ready for bed. She climbed under the covers and turned off the light. But she had trouble sleeping. She tossed and turned all night. And when she did sleep, she dreamed of a scary face chasing her.

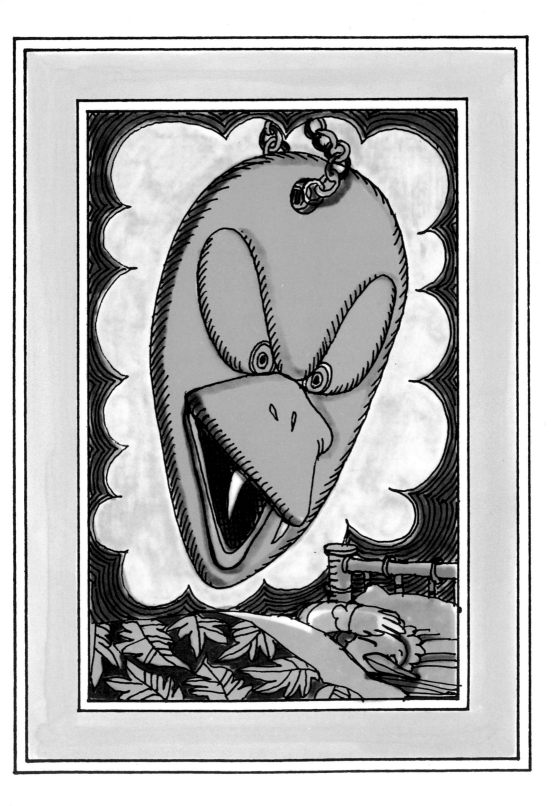

When morning finally came, Miss Mallard had made up her mind. She was certain that the carved scary face belonged to one of three suspects. But which suspect? Then she had a plan. She put on a bulky sweater, a cap, and dark glasses to disguise herself as a delivery person. After that she wrapped the keychain in a box and tied the box with a ribbon.

"Now for my first delivery," she said as she left the inn.

Miss Mallard's first stop was at the home of Clyde Pochard, her first suspect. She rang the doorbell. Pochard himself opened the door.

"I have a delivery for you from Norman's Department Store," said Miss Mallard in a disguised voice.

"I didn't order anything from there," said Pochard.

Miss Mallard insisted that he open the box to see if he had placed the order. Pochard opened the box and took out the carved scary face.

"Why would I order this silly keychain?" he said angrily. "Take it back. I've never seen it before."

Pochard slammed the door.

"Too bad," thought Miss Mallard. "I thought the keychain might be for his bulldozer."

Miss Mallard's next stop was at Horace Shoveller's digging site.

"I have a delivery for you from Manny-Ki's Antique Shop," said Miss Mallard.

"For me?" said Horace Shoveller. "I wonder what it could be?"

He opened the box and his beak dropped.

"What *is* this ugly thing?" he cried. "A keychain? *Really*! This is not for me."

He tossed the box back to Miss Mallard.

"I'm sorry about the mistake," said Miss Mallard. "Perhaps the store thought the carving of the scary face would interest you."

"Never!" said Horace Shoveller angrily. "I only collect rare art. Take it back."

With that Miss Mallard went on her way and thought, "That clears the second suspect."

Miss Mallard's last stop was at Joe
Scaup's shack on the wharf. She found
him packing a rowboat.

"Going somewhere?" asked Miss
Mallard.

"None of your business," said Joe
Scaup.

"Well, I have a package for you from
Sadie's Curio Shop," said Miss Mallard.

"What are you talking about?" said Joe
Scaup. "I've never heard of Sadie's Shop."

Miss Mallard insisted that he open the
box. Joe Scaup removed the lid and
looked inside. He saw the keychain and
gasped. Miss Mallard knew at once that
it was his.

"Where did you get this?" he yelled.
"Who sent you?"

"So it was *you* who took the stone!" said Miss Mallard as she ripped off her dark glasses.

"Great Davy Jones's Locker!" cried Joe Scaup. "Miss Mallard, herself! How did you know I took it?"

Miss Mallard answered, "I suspected you when I saw the face carved from a shark's tooth. It is a sailor's hobby to make carvings like this. But like all good ducktectives I had to make sure, so I checked out the other suspects first. I knew the keychain didn't belong to any of the villagers because they live in grass huts and don't need keys. The jig is up. You had better return the stone and forget this nonsense. Where is it?"

"It's in my canvas bag," said Joe Scaup. "I should have known you would find me out. That's why I chased you in the jungle when I remembered about the keychain. I wanted to get it back before it was too late. But you were too quick for me."

"So it *was* you in the jungle last night," said Miss Mallard. "But why did you take the stone?"

"I know plenty of people who would buy it from me," said Joe Scaup. "I could have made myself some real money. AND I CAN STILL DO IT!"

Just then he grabbed a rope and hurled himself forward at Miss Mallard.

"I'm going to leave you tied up in my shack while I row away with the stone to another island," he said.

"I was ready for this," said Miss Mallard.

In a flash, she leaped out of the way. Then she reached into her knitting bag and pulled out the conch shell she had found. She held it up as she had seen Naku-Naku do on the beach and blew hard, "Aaaawooooooo!"

"Cut that out!" cried Joe Scaup.

He was too late. Everyone came running from all over and headed directly for the wharf. Even the police came this time. Naku-Naku and Mori-Hi were the first to get there.

"I've recovered the stone," said Miss Mallard. "It's in Joe Scaup's canvas bag."

Naku-Naku and Mori-Hi opened the bag and sure enough the stone was there. Then Miss Mallard told the police everything and Joe Scaup was taken away to jail.

As everyone was leaving to take the stone back to the beach and replace it on the pedestal, Clyde Pochard came tearing along in his bulldozer. This time he narrowly missed hitting a policeman and was given a ticket. And another ticket for driving on the beach. And still another for putting people's lives in jeopardy.

"That's a lot of tickets," said Naku-Naku to Miss Mallard. "It will be a relief not to see him and his bulldozer on the beach."

"And one less risk for me when I go surfing," said Miss Mallard.

"Which reminds me," said Mori-Hi, "SURF'S UP!"

The three of them ran to get their surfboards.

"Oh, my," said Miss Mallard looking at the surf. "I've never ridden waves that big before."

"You can do it, Miss Mallard," said Naku-Naku. "You can do anything!"

And so the three of them jumped into the water on their surfboards and paddled out to sea.